I0672755

Devil's Halo

Helen C. Ayers

Helen C. Ayers

Printed in the United States of America

ISBN: 978-1-7366760-1-1

DEDICATION

I would like to thank the many police in Southern Indiana,
Nashville and Bloomington especially, for trusting me to tell not only a
good story, but a factually correct story as well.

Helen C. Ayers

Helen C. Ayers

CONTENTS

Helen C. Ayers

Helen C. Ayers

ACKNOWLEDGMENTS

The information provided in this book is entirely fictional, all characters are the author's own as well as the fact the "Eden Ranch" does not exist except in the author's brain but which these events could be taken as actually happening except for the following information.

Helen C. Ayers

CHAPTER ONE

Billy Kent did not know what a difference today would make in his life. He was simply too young, at eight-years-old, to know that after today his life would never again be the same.

Young Billy had spent his entire life living with just his mother for company—he did not have a daddy—had never had one as far as he knew. But recently his mom had been having some problems. He thought her problems had to do with drugs which he had learned a lot about at school from the nice young policeman, Jim Morris, from the Just Say No drug program.

Too many times lately Billy had awakened in the morning to find that he had spent the entire night alone again or with one of his "uncles" babysitting him and he was terrified of being alone—bad men come sometime when you are alone after dark.

It was on those lonely mornings when he had to pour his own milk—sometimes watered down with tears—over his dry cereal before heading out to get on the school bus that he sometimes thought of ending his own young life. But each morning when this happened he would stoically eat those little round circles of soggy oats.

For his school lunch Billy spread a thin layer of peanut butter and jelly on two slices of white bread, wrapped it in plastic wrap, and got ready for school. The jelly jar was almost empty. Would his mom remember and bring him some more if he used it all up? He loved his PB&J sandwiches so it was crucial that she bring him some more jelly. Would she remember that blackberry was his favorite flavor of jelly?

What was the use of living he would sometimes think to himself? Nobody would care if I just died. Nobody loves me. But Billy knew deep down in his heart that his mom really did love him and needed him but she had come to depend upon drugs so much lately maybe she no longer thought much about him. She had not said the important three little words to him in a long time. Billy still loved her with all his heart but he wished he could be like all the other young kids he knew in school.

He really, badly wanted both a daddy and a mommy who loved him and maybe a little brother or sister to play with and watch over, but he knew that that would never happen for him. He would always be alone. He did not even know who his father had been—a trucker passing through town maybe--who had left his mom when she got pregnant with young Billy. His mom just said he never had a daddy, but every little boy had a daddy somewhere, he thought to himself. "I wish I knew who mine was and where he is now. Maybe he would love me and want me."

In another home across the railroad tracks in the same tiny Midwestern town known as Stoneville lived another young child, ten-year-old Sally Quinn. She too was being neglected by her single mother who had also fallen upon hard times recently.

In order to make ends meet after losing her job at the car parts factory that had closed down and moved to Mexico, and unable to find another well-paying factory job to support herself and her child, the mother had been cooking amphetamines (meth, or crank, as it was called in street lingo) and selling that to drug users to earn enough money to keep her and her little girl in food and clothing.

Sally hated the stink of ammonia which was one of the main ingredients in the making of meth. Each afternoon when she returned home from school and stepped down from the school bus steps she would lift her head into the air and breathe deeply. If the ammonia smell was especially strong, she knew that her mother was cooking another batch of the drug in the little shed out behind their house. Meth was the drug of choice of young Billy's mother and many others, including Sally's mother although neither of these children knew much about each other or the other's' mother.

The children recognized each other from school because the school was very small, having just 125 students in kindergarten through six grades. But because Sally was a couple of years older than Billy she was in the fifth grade while Billy was only in the second grade so they were not friends exactly, but they recognized each other in passing and were linked together through their mom's drug making and use.

At school today these two children sat nearly spellbound as they listened to the young policeman make his speech to them as they gathered in the auditorium about saying no to drugs. Today's lesson contained a small bit of information he had never shared with the children before. Today he told them who to call if someone offered to sell them drugs or if they knew anyone who was making and selling it and what they should do about it as he passed a small white card to each child.

2

This young man, Officer Jim Morris, gave the children a phone number to call to report any drug information. "Just call us, you don't have to give us your name, and we will look into the situation," Officer Morris promised them.

Both children carefully placed the cards this officer had given them into their front britches pocket. Both would take this card out and read it over many times in the next few hours until both had memorized the phone number for Officer Morris. Would he really come and help them if they called that number, each wondered?

Later that afternoon Sally's mother handed her daughter $10 and asked Sally to run to the nearby Everything's a Buck or Less store, and buy some more coffee filters. The store was only two blocks away in this small rural town so it should be safe enough for Sally to walk alone on this small errand for her mother. Sally agreed to do her mother's errand and took the money and ran outside, skipping merrily down the sidewalk. It would be the last time Sally's mother would ever again see her child alive.

Thus it was, that Sally knew from seeing and smelling the ammonia that her mother used to cook the meth exactly what it was she was seeing and smelling as she walked by the open door of a run-down apartment house and glanced inside to see three guys doing the same thing her mother did that she recognized what they were doing. They were making drugs, she thought to herself, then she took off running toward the nearby discount store.

Once Sally had bought the coffee filters for her mom and carefully placed the change into her pocket, she picked up the small sack, walked outside the store and saw a pay telephone hanging in a small alcove against the wall.

Stopping momentarily to think about what she was doing, she removed a quarter from her pocket, lifted the receiver and dropped the quarter into the coin slot and dialed the phone number of Officer Morris that she had memorized. The phone rang and rang on the other end, but Officer Morris did not answer.

Perhaps he was instructing another group of youngsters about saying no to drugs, Sally thought, as she replaced the phone on its hook. To watch her one would think her call had been completed and this worried more than one person.

One of the men she had observed making meth inside the run-down apartment had been dispatched by the other two men to keep an eye on Sally. This man had seen her go inside the store and come out with a small sack. He had watched her make a phone call and speculated about who she might be calling. He walked back to the apartment and reported to the other two men what he had seen.

Unknown to all was the fact that a second man had also seen Sally go into the store and then make the phone call. This man had been stalking Sally at her mom's house after school for some time now. He knew that her mother often sent Sally on errands alone. This second man decided to do something about it.

This fairly handsome man knocked on Sally's mom's door and when she came to see who it was, he forcibly removed her from the home and led her through a small patch of woods, and placed her inside his old white beat-up pickup truck.

He had all intentions of raping her then killing her, why waste a victim, he thought, and she would be out of young Sally's life and out of my way with that young girl.

After a short drive to a marshy area to the west of the little town, he pulled her and dragged her when he had to way back into the swampy area. After raping her repeatedly and beating on the woman with his fists, he throttled her with his bare hands until she went limp.

The man did not like to rape older women with the larger breasts. He preferred his victims to be young, nubile and tiny breasted. Rarely could he consummate sex with an adult woman, but preyed on children instead, but this one would do.

Lighting a cigarette, he inhaled it until it was about half smoked and then applied the still hot cigarette to one of her breasts, burning her severely and leaving her body to the turtles and other wildlife.

He saw Sally walking home and drove his old pickup truck up beside her. He leaned out his driver's side window, and asked her if she had seen his lost puppy, as he described it for her.

"It is a small beagle and he is so cute with floppy ears and he is black, brown and white," he told Sally. "Have you seen him? His name is Sparky."

"Can you help me look for my dog?" he asked her.

Sally knew she was not supposed to talk to strangers. Her mom had lectured her more than once about that and Officer Morris had also spoken about not talking to strangers one day on a visit to her school.

But this guy had lost his puppy and Sally loved little dogs and wished she had one of her very own. She always asked for a puppy for Christmas but her mother had never brought one home to her, so she was very interested in looking for this man's little dog.

He was neatly dressed and appeared to be clean and about the same age as her mother. Surely it would not hurt to help him look for his little puppy as he drove slowly along the streets of her hometown, and he had promised to buy her an ice cream cone at the nearby Dairy Queen after they found Sparky, so Sally crawled into the passenger seat of the old truck.

After cautioning her gently to fasten her seat belt securely, the man, who told her his name was John, began driving slowly away. "You watch and I'll

4

drive, and we can cover more ground that way," John told Sally as she laid the package of coffee filters onto the seat beside her and started searching for the man's lost dog. Suddenly and without warning as the man turned a nearby corner onto another street, the man sped up and took off north out of town.

Now Sally was becoming scared. "Hey, where are you going?" she asked John. "My mommy would be mad if I left our town with you without asking her for permission."

For an answer John—the man Billy's mother had thought she could trust with her son when she needed a sitter—leaned across the seat and slapped Sally hard across her face, making her start to cry. "Just shut up," John replied.

"Stop, I want to get out. I do not want to help you look for your dog anymore," Sally pleaded as she wiped blood from her split lip, but John ignored her as he sped up the highway toward a fairly large town just up the road.

Sally saw the direction they were headed and realized she might be able to get help when they got to the more populated area. She made plans to scream if she saw anyone whom she thought might help her. But just before they got inside the city limits, John made Sally crouch down onto the floorboard so she could not see outside and no one could see her inside his truck. Sally was now becoming really, really frightened.

Finally, John told her she could get back up into the seat. When Sally got back up from the floorboard, she realized they had passed through the larger town entirely and were once again out into open country, and still headed north.

There was an interstate highway just north of this town where there was an on-ramp for the interstate. Beside that on-ramp, there was a small park where a lake had been created during the building of the big highway to bring the roadway up out of the flood plain. The park had picnic tables, trash barrels, was blacktopped and had a rustic outdoor restroom without a water supply. John pulled off the highway into this small rest area.

The area had been nearly inaccessible to local fishermen and folks just wanting a place to play outdoors because it had been taken over by undesirable men who came there to make a drug or homosexual connection. Arrests were frequent and many but Sally did not know that. She had never been to this park before.

No one else was using the park today except John and Sally; the old white pickup was the only vehicle in the parking lot and John had parked it behind the restroom where it was not visible from the roadway, being further camouflaged by the trees.

Sally asked John if she could use the restroom and he said yes so they both got down from the pickup and she ran towards the bathroom hoping to get inside and lock the door before John could get there.

But just as Sally got inside the restroom she heard someone entering behind her and quickly spun around to see that John had followed her inside. Now she was scared nearly to death because John had a very funny look on his face. Sally already knew that that particular look did not bode well for her because several of the "uncles" who came home with her mom, looked at her in the same way and she became even more frightened.

"What do you want?" Sally squeaked as she saw John was loosening his belt and unzipping his pants. He had already kicked his shoes off and he kept looking at her with that stupid expression on his face as he continued undressing.

Sally noted to herself that the door was now locked behind them. She was alone, locked in with this stranger.

"Please, don't hurt me," she begged.

John just grinned lewdly as he told her to take her clothing off.

"No, I won't do it," Sally screamed. "You can't make me do that."

But she soon came to understand that John could make her do that.

John merely took another step toward her, then reached out and grabbed her blouse at the neck, yanking down hard until the entire front was now torn open. Sally, who was just beginning to grow a bosom was so embarrassed she could have died when she looked down and saw her tiny naked buds.

John then slapped her hard again and knocked her to her knees.

"Please let me go," Sally begged John. "I will not tell anyone what you have done."

"I know you won't tell anyone. I'll see to that," John told her as he reached for her again.

Sally tried to evade him, but she simply was not strong enough or fast enough to get away from this very strong man.

John continued to slap and beat on Sally until she could no longer resist or scream for help before she passed out. John then tore the remaining clothing from her small body and did vile and unspeakable things to her. Finally, placing his hands around her young throat and pressing down with strong fingers until he felt her body go lifeless in his hands he ejaculated.

This depraved dog then replaced his clothing carefully and nonchalantly lit a cigarette. When he had completed smoking the cigarette and savoring his rape acts and had calmed down, he placed the lit end of the cigarette against one of her small budding breasts and held it there to extinguish the flame, enjoying the smell of burning flesh. Young Sally had shared the same fate as her mother on the same day by the same perpetrator.

Without making a sound after he had re-dressed, he very carefully slid the very rudimentary lock back, looked outside to verify that no one else was in the area then he stooped and picked up the young girl's limp body.

He carried her small body about 50 yards away and threw it down on the edge of a small creek which ran alongside the park and then meandered through some farm fields toward the nearby river. He laughed as he took his foot and kicked her body down into the water of the slow-flowing, muddy creek as though it were a bit of flotsam washed up during a flood.

John remained in place to smoke one more cigarette as he watched her body begin to slide out into the cold, icy water and start to move slowly downstream. Dropping the cigarette butt to the ground he walked back to his pickup truck, threw out the bag containing the coffee filters she had carried and drove away.

"This was so easy to rape and kill both mom and daughter, I will have to do this again," Thus was born a serial killer in a small Midwestern town.

CHAPTER TWO

Meanwhile, after sending Sally to the store for the coffee filters, and when she had not returned promptly, Sally's mother had become quite concerned about her daughter's absence.

It had now been almost two hours since she had sent her young daughter to the store for the coffee filters and she still had not returned home. Perhaps she had gone on to the playground to play with some friends or something.

Worried, Mrs. Quinn had placed a call to the state police post which was only a mile away. Her latest batch of meth had finished cooking now and the stench of meth seemed to have dissipated.

She, too, would have been surprised to learn the same man who had kidnapped her daughter those two hours past would now be the same man who had knocked at her door. But for her, she would never know that.

A man, finding the door unlocked, had opened the door and slipped quietly into the room where Sally's mother had been placing her phone call to the police.

He slipped up behind Mrs. Quinn and bashed her head in with a heavy object he had brought with him, killing her nearly instantly.

He then dragged and carried her to his old pickup truck which he had parked on a side road not far from the Quinn residence and drove her to the swampy area just outside the town to the west.

Hating to miss an opportunity that presented itself so easily he half dragged, half carried Mrs. Quinn way back in the swampy area where he raped her in all manner possible, smoked his cigarette and burned her left breast with it.

He then left her body for the critters to take care of and went back to his residence, satisfied with having had both mother and daughter in one day to do his bidding.

But this afternoon as she was speaking to the dispatcher, the young mother had had time to explain about her daughter going missing after a short walk to the local store two hours before.

The dispatcher put the mother through to State Police Detective Darren Andrews who took down the relevant missing child information from the distraught mother. He then advised the mother that he would be stopping by her house very shortly for a picture of her daughter so that he could put out an Amber Alert to get the public's help in finding her.

But Detective Andrews was held up for a few minutes and arrived too late to save Mrs. Quinn. The front door was still unlocked when he arrived. He pushed on it and it opened. He called out to Mrs. Quinn but she did not answer his call.

This was very curious to Detective Andrews since he had told her he would see her very shortly. "I wonder why she is not at home," he thought to himself.

After looking through the entire home he found that she really was not at home. As he was leaving the home he saw a picture in a frame sitting on a small table near the door. He picked up the picture to see it was of a young girl, about Sally's age.

He took the picture with him and went to the elementary school and asked the teachers there the name of the girl. Learning it really was a picture of the girl, Sally, he needed to use for the Amber Alert, he went back to his police post and put the Amber Alert out to the public using her picture.

The Amber Alert was created after another young girl had gone missing and was later found dead. The law making it mandatory for it to be issued had been passed by the state's legislature some years ago. It had helped locate several children, most of whom had been taken by a non-custodial parent and most of those children had been found safe and returned to the proper custodial parent.

Once an Amber Alert had been issued there were electronic flashing signs along all interstate roadways in the state advising motorists to watch for the missing child. Television programming would be interrupted so that reporters could show a picture of a missing child, give her description and the description of any vehicle she might be riding in.

Detective Andrews also touched base with Sallianne Carmichael who was an ace reporter for a local weekly newspaper who had worked with Detective Andrews on several cases in the past. Both detective and reporter had a healthy respect for the other's talents. Detective Andrews knew Sallianne would do everything in her power to write a balanced and accurate story about this believed stranger-abduction rather than a non-custodial parental abduction of a child.

When Detective Andrews had first met Sallianne she had just come on board the newspaper as a reporter. Now, upon the retirement of her editor, she now owned the weekly newspaper and was doing a super job. They had covered numerous felony crimes together successfully.

The search for young Sally was carried on all throughout that evening and long into the night by volunteers and police agencies from several counties.

But by daylight it was becoming more and more apparent that something very dire may have happened to Sally, and perhaps her mother too, since she had not reappeared and no one knew where she had gone and why she left her house instead of waiting for Detective Andrew. More and more volunteers came in to search for Sally.

At school the next day the children were advised by counselors that one of their friends had disappeared but were told that the police and many others were searching for her. The remaining students were counseled if they were upset and were warned again about talking to any strangers in the area.

Across town, young Billy had also placed a telephone call to the same number Sally had called but he got lucky and Officer Morris answered his call.

Billy told Officer Morris about his mother being missing and told him that he had spent the previous night alone.

Officer Morris promised he would be right there to help him and asked Billy to just sit tight until he got to his house. "Don't let in any strangers," he advised Billy.

Billy promised he would not let anyone in he did not know until the officer arrived.

By this time, too, Officer Morris had been advised about the missing Sally and her mother and was very concerned about Billy so he hurried to Billy's house to see what was going on.

Arriving on the scene he found young Billy alone and without food. Officer Morris alerted the state police and advised Detective Darren Andrews about the call from Billy since he knew Detective Andrews was already on the case of the missing Quinn family members. He also called the child protective services of the local police agency and reported what he had found and asked that someone come and help Billy.

A very nice middle-aged woman named Millie came immediately and assured Billy she would take care of him.

Officer Morris allowed Billy to leave the home with Millie who said she would see that he was placed in a responsible foster care program until his mother could be located.

When Billy got to the office of the Child Protection Agency, he listened as Millie placed a call to a foster home on his behalf.

From listening to her side of the conversation he learned that the home had space for him and learned he would be taken there straightaway.

With some uneasiness, Billy went with Millie to this home in the country.

Upon his arrival he found there were many children just like him living in this home which appeared to consist of about 50 parents and 175 children. The name of the place was Children of Eden Ranch.

There were horses to ride, orchards of fruit and gardens with plenty of food to eat. Billy saw a basketball court where several young people were having a one-on-one hoops game. A nearby soccer field had more children playing there and many others standing on the sidelines cheering for children wearing either yellow or red t-shirts to indicate the different teams.

Billy thought he just might like to live here but knew he would really miss his mommy.

He was taken inside a big home and introduced to the top Daddy "Tom" and Mommy "Marie", who made an effort to make him feel at home.

First, he was scrubbed clean in a big tub of warm, soapy water, given fresh clothing and then he was placed before a table heaped with lots of good smelling food.

Billy ate until he could not hold another bite before his little head started nodding. But he had been just so hungry since it had been yesterday noon at school that he had eaten a hot meal.

Seeing that he was starting to go to sleep and knowing he would sleep the night through, Billy was placed in a clean bed and the covers were pulled up over his skinny little chest.

It was the next morning upon arrival at school that he discovered the girl, Sally Quinn, had gone missing.

"That could have been me," Billy thought to himself.

CHAPTER THREE

The foster home had been in existence only about two years and was supported entirely by donations from church and religious groups. Great hopes were expected by these devout followers from this new venture.

Those families living nearby the ranch had tried repeatedly to block its inception.

They claimed the county officials responsible for approving it had violated the trust of their constituents by approving this type of development in a single-family neighborhood.

Many did not trust or believe in the director, expecting vile things to happen to the children at his hands or at the hands of those volunteers he accepted to be mommies and daddies. But after two years, none of their expectations had happened. Could all of these good, concerned people living near the ranch be in error?

Still the residents living nearby the home center did not believe that the man was as pure and sanctimonious as he claimed to be.

"Nobody is that good or perfect and works without pay to rear this many children," they would say.

But so far, there had been no supportable evidence of either abuse or neglect.

One prominent neighbor said she would be keeping her camera and zoom lens at the ready to document any wrong-doings occurring in this compound. She had even hired an electrician to mount a video camera on a tall pole and point it at the compound to record the comings and goings of its inhabitants.

"I'll be watching every move this man makes. When I start seeing young girls with swollen bellies full of babies, I'm calling in the FBI," she told anyone who would listen.

At first, Billy thought he had died and gone straight to heaven. He loved this place but he sure missed his mommy.

"I wish she would come and get me," he cried to himself every night. But his Mommy could not ever come back for him. It would appear that Billy had been abandoned. Now he had neither a father nor a mother, but he began trying to make a few friends among the other children in his new "home."

When Sallianne heard that young Billy had been placed in this home she became very concerned. Billy was the first child she had known personally who had been placed in the care of this very charismatic man and his wife, a board-certified child psychologist.

Sallianne had become very wary of this couple when she was introduced to their half dozen adopted sons when the couple had stopped by her office to talk with her about doing a story on their ranch.

Their boys appeared to be physically fit and healthy, but their mental attitude deeply disturbed Sallianne.

The mother introduced the first child and told him to introduce himself to Sallianne. She did this by nodding to him and the youngest child stated, "Hello, Mrs. Carmichael, my name is Thomas."

Wanting to appear friendly towards the abnormally quiet eight-year-old boy, Sallianne replied. "Hi Tommy, how are you?"

Tommy responded again by saying, "My name is Thomas," with absolutely no inflection in his voice.

Sallianne knew by the time the mother had nodded at her second son to introduce himself, that she should not shorten James to Jimmy, nor say Dick instead of Richard. Each boy used the exact same words with no inflection in their voices except for speaking his own full first name, to this new acquaintance.

"This is really weird," Sallianne thought to herself. "These boys speak only when the mother nods her head at them. Am I just imagining this?" she wondered. But others had said the same thing to Sallianne.

The family soon left but Sallianne was disturbed for a long time by this very strange family.

"Do they want to turn all these children belonging to others into this kind of robotic behavior," she wondered.

From that day forward, Sallianne watched any news releases that came into her office from this religious ranch.

She had visions of Waco and Guyana and the disastrous outcome of those Edenish compounds at the hands of other men who claimed to be the next things to God.

"Well, let's give them a chance. Maybe you are worrying about nothing," Detective Andrews told Sallianne.

And it was into this ranch that the Child Protective Services had placed her young acquaintance, Billy.

Sallianne explained her concerns to Detective Andrews when he stopped by her office to discuss the disappearance of the young girl the day before from this sleepy little Midwestern town.

"Have you found any evidence of Billy's mother," she asked Darren.

"Not a speck of evidence. It is like this little kid has always lived alone," the trooper said. "There were none of her clothes inside the house, just the little boy's clothing. All the food available to him had already been eaten. I just don't understand how a mother could do that to her child.

"I am going to look for any accident or homicide victims from reports on file in my office. Perhaps I can find a clue to her whereabouts from that," Detective Andrews told Sallianne.

"Well, keep me posted," she responded.

CHAPTER FOUR

Time went on and young Billy settled into his new home and attended school. He made a few friends but still cried himself to sleep every night wondering where his Mommy could be.

On a fall afternoon that was bright with sunshine and falling leaves he learned that Daddy Tom was leaving for the day. He was going to be calling on several churches in the area asking for donations to maintain his ranch.

Daddy Tom told his wife, known to the children as Mommy Marie, that he was going to take young Billy with him as far as the boy's previous home and see if he could find any evidence of the boy's missing Mommy.

"Perhaps the police have overlooked something that Billy will recognize," he explained to his wife.

"That is a good idea. No one except Billy would know if something was out of the ordinary," she agreed.

It had now been a while since Billy had been brought to the Children of Eden ranch and Daddy Tom had not been away from the ranch for any length of time. Daddy Tom was feeling like he needed to call on friendly church groups again. Inviting Billy and the barn keeper, Johnathan Coats, to join him in the old white battered pickup truck, he made sure that the boy was securely fastened into his seat belt and started off to return the boy to his former home.

"Maybe I can find your Mommy for you or find out what happened to her," he told young Billy.

Daddy Tom spent most of that morning and much of the afternoon calling upon church groups as he had explained to his wife he would be doing. As he met with the various groups he offered prayers and talked about God and told the groups how much he appreciated their monetary offers.

He had left Johnathan at the feed mill to oversee the grinding of their grain for the camp's horses. He left young Billy at his mommy's house when he saw someone on the porch and assumed it was someone Billy knew well.

But once Billy got to the porch he realized that it was not his mommy standing there but one of the "uncles" his mommy was always bringing home with her.

This scared Billy and he made an attempt to run back across the lawn to Daddy Tom's vehicle, but Daddy Tom had already left the area. The man on the porch was a man who had sexually assaulted him several times in the past when Billy had been left in his care while his mommy had to leave the home for a while. And Billy was terrified of him.

There was on old white, rusty pickup truck sitting nearby across a small span of trees and the man on the porch forced young Billy to get in the truck. His door was immediately locked, and Billy was made to put on his seat belt. The man surely didn't want police stopping him for allowing a child to ride in his vehicle without a seat belt on. He had far better uses for this young boy.

The assailant followed the same route he had taken with the young girl, Sally Quinn, and this boy would get the same treatment.

As soon as they arrived at the deserted park he and Billy went inside the outdoor toilet. Then he undid his belt buckle and his trousers and made young Billy do the same, then he vented his tortured mind's activity on this young boy's body. Billy screamed and cried all the time it was going on but the Uncle slapped him repeatedly fearing someone would drive into the parking lot and hear him.

When at last the assault on Billy was over, young Billy was dead and the assailant lighted a cigarette, which seemed to have become his trademark murder mark. Holding the half-smoked cigarette in his hand, he leaned over the body of little Billy and applied the hot end of the cigarette to one of his flat paps on the tiny chest.

He had suffered the same fate as young Sally Quinn. The assailant was exhausted by this time and still needed to be rid of the body.

He noted there was a metal waste can in one corner of the room that had a lid on it. He removed the lid and dumped Billy's body into that, put the cover back on, and lit another cigarette. He had had a marvelous time today but he would miss this child.

The assailant could have used him several more times because it was assumed by the police that his mommy had abandoned him and could no longer protect Billy.

Daddy Tom returned to the COE and explained to his wife that he had left Billy at his old home to visit for the day when he had seen someone standing on the front porch and assumed it was someone Billy already knew.

While Billy was visiting, Daddy Tom had called on the churches and Johnathan saw to the milling of our grain. He had explained to Billy that he would return later and pick him up again. But when I returned to pick him up this afternoon there was no one there he continued his recitation to Mommy Marie of this day's activities.

I didn't know where Jonathan had gone and I didn't see him or anyone else at the home either.

I figured the mom had left again, taking young Billy with her. So, I don't believe we will see him again, Daddy Tom finished.

His wife responded by saying that she was glad that Billy had found his mother or someone who cared about him, but said she would miss him a lot and, oh, Jonathan came back early and said he had caught a ride back up here with someone else.

"I really will miss Billy," Mommy Marie said.

"Yeah, I will miss the little guy a lot also," her husband responded. "I better call his school in the morning and explain why he is not in school.

Don't forget to remind me if I get busy. I drove to the state police post and told them about thinking his mom had taken off with the boy. They said they would watch for her and let me know if she is spotted. I didn't know anything else to do so I came on home."

"OK, I'll remind you. Now are you ready for bed? I have missed you today," she said as she rubbed his thigh.

"Yeah, but I am so tired I'll probably go to sleep as soon as my head hits my pillow," he replied, and he did just that.

The weeks rolled by and several more children came to the ranch and others left to be returned to their natural parents.

Daddy Tom always took each child up into his old truck, made sure they were buckled in securely, told his wife goodbye and drove away.

Daddy Tom always maintained that he wanted to be the one to return these wonderful young kids to their natural parents. "I just think that is the best way to do it and I believe it will further generate funds when people realize what good care their children have had here at Children of Eden."

Mommy Marie nodded her head; she always agreed with Daddy Tom.

CHAPTER FIVE

The search for Sally or her killer continued at a frantic pace.

Detective Andrews had taken an anonymous telephone call from a man who talked about seeing the young girl in an old white pickup truck the day of her disappearance. The driver of the truck was described as a well-dressed slightly older man.

Detective Andrews had made a door-to-door search knocking on all the doors in Sally's hometown, trying to get a handle on who the driver could have been or learn if anyone knew of an old white pickup that fit the description he had.

Several of the residents told Detective Andrews the only pickup that had seen that matched that description belonged to Daddy Tom and everyone knew how kind he was. He was in town often, picking up supplies and stuff for his ranch. But all agreed this very kind and Godly man could not be the one responsible for any child's disappearance. "It must be someone else," they told Detective Andrews and he had to agree.

About three blocks from Sally's home he knocked on the door of a rather run-down apartment building after he had seen an old white pickup truck parked outside the building which had one wheel set up on concrete blocks.

The door was opened by a very nervous man who held the door open only about the length of a safety chain. He refused to let Detective Andrews enter his home. Noticing the suspicious nature of the man, Detective Andrews flashed his badge and demanded that he open the door and admit him.

Finally, the nervous man closed the door briefly and removed the safety chain to admit Detective Andrews.

"What are you so nervous and scared of?" Detective Andrews questioned the man.

"I'm not nervous," he responded as he shifted from one foot to the other.

"Yes, you are. What are you hiding?" the officer asked.

"What kind of vehicle do you drive? Is that your white pickup truck out front?" the man was asked.

"I've got an old white pickup truck that runs sometimes and sometimes it doesn't; right now, it is not running and is setting out there on a block. It needs a new tire," he responded.

"Were you driving it on March 6 of this year when the little girl living just down the street disappeared?" he questioned.

"Probably," he replied. "Why do you want to know that?"

"Because she was seen in the company of a man inside an older model white pickup truck by several people around town," he was told.

The man being questioned suddenly and without reason burst into tears, saying, "I didn't mean to hurt her," he cried.

Detective Andrews knew that he had finally found his man and advised him of his rights. "You know the routine I'm sure, stand leaning with your hands against the wall while I frisk you for weapons.

The officer did not find any weapons on the scruffy man so he handcuffed him with his hands behind his back and repeated the Miranda warning to his prisoner.

The suspect was taken to the county jail and pushed roughly into a holding cell.

Detective Andrews and various other members of the law enforcement community set up a time for the suspect to be questioned.

He was brought from his cell at 3 a.m. and placed in a small room that held one desk and three chairs. There were no windows and no other amenities except one small mirror and a tape recorder sitting in the center of the desk inside the room. The room smelled of stale sweat and greasy food.

Detective Andrews flipped on the light switch as he entered the interrogation room, the suspect never knew that he was on camera and that several other officers were in the adjoining room listening to the interview and watching the action.   There had been a tiny hidden camera mounted behind a screw hole in the plate cover.   To make sure that no problems would arise later, the suspect was again advised of his rights on camera and asked if he wanted his attorney to be present.

The suspect said he understood the Miranda warning and did not need his attorney to be present. It took the experienced detective only thirty minutes to get a full confession from the scummy guy.

He admitted he had picked the little girl up, but said he did not know her name until he read it in the newspaper the day after her disappearance.

He told his interrogators how he had driven out to the "Bottoms"—a large portion of land nearby the town that had many small creeks running through it that stayed at flood stage most of the year because it was so low in elevation. He said he had raped and then killed Sally and disposed of her body out there in the Bottoms.

"Do you remember where you left her? Can you take us to the spot so we can find her body and bring it home for a proper burial?" he was asked.

"I'm sure I can," he responded.

The cops loaded him in the backseat of a patrol car that had heavy wire mesh between the two compartments and no door handles on the back doors and set off for the Bottoms area.

Detective Andrews continued questioning his suspect all the way out to the Bottoms area. "Did you leave her body in the water or leave it in a field or what?"

"I pushed her into the creek and left her there," the prime suspect said.

He described in detail the area and what it looked like where he had left her body.

After hours of driving through this area that had many tiny, one-lane gravel roads running through it and green water standing even with the roadway alongside the roads, the suspect could not find where he had left Sally's body. "Every road looks just like all the others," the suspect said.

Finally, the cops, giving up on learning anything useful from this suspect, returned him to the jail.

The next morning, he was arraigned before Judge Frank Rosenbaum and charged with abduction, rape and first-degree murder, even though no body had yet been found.

By this time several weeks had gone by so the chances of anyone finding the young girl's body in that boggy area was very slim, but a caravan of eager volunteers agreed to spend as long as it took them to search for and find her body.

Thus, the next morning about 50-75 volunteers showed up at the police station to begin their search.

Two people were assigned to each team with an area of about one mile in length to search. All the volunteers had to stay with a partner and each of them was given an orange reflective vest to wear for safety reasons and for identification. While searching, they would walk along the roadside, peering into the water-filled canals alongside the road.

Once they had walked their mile and met up with the two searchers coming from the opposite direction, and when they found a place to cross over to the other side, they repeated the process back to the point of beginning. That way if one searcher had missed seeing a clue, perhaps the other person would discover something useful on the return trip.

But after hours and hours of intensive searching, not a single clue was found. They found several old tires, and lots of discarded junk but no girl's body.

"There just isn't anything out here for us to find," one said to his partner. "I'm wondering if he is being truthful with Detective Andrews."

But not giving up, the next day the same partners shared another mile of the roadway that had been gone over by two others the day before.

Again, not a single clue was found by any of the searchers. The searchers again found tons of discarded household waste and automotive tires, but nothing even remotely that could be considered evidence of murder.

Hearing this news, Detective Andrews decided to question his suspect once again. He knew from past experience that hardly any suspects could be believed one hundred percent.

But by the time he decided to re-question the suspect, the suspect had decided not to talk anymore to anyone about the case.

An attorney had been appointed for him by the judge during the arraignment and the attorney advised him to just keep his mouth shut and remain mum.

That is exactly what the suspect did. He would not utter one word.

CHAPTER SIX

In the meanwhile, other members of the state police post were busily preparing to conduct a surprise raid on the little park up by the interstate hoping to catch some perverts who had been reported seen there several times. They never dreamed what they would actually find.

"Let's go up this afternoon and see how many we can round up," one rookie said to the other as they rushed outside and jumped into their patrol car.

Arriving at the park they realized there was only one street in an out of it which made things much easier for just the two patrolmen to cover the exit.

But when they got to the park there was not one car or pickup truck sitting in the parking lot. The entire park was empty.

"Darn, I believe someone told these guys we were coming."

"Well, let's take a quick look-see anyway and see if we can tell how much activity has been going on around here. We get a lot of complaints from this area."

They first checked out the outer area around the bathroom then walked over and stood looking down at the nearly stagnant water of a tiny stream.

At this point they had not looked inside either of the bathrooms.

"Wow, what is that thing I am looking at out there," one Rookie asked his partner pointing a finger at the object. "It looks like a body or something. Maybe we better call this in."

Returning to their car, they radioed their headquarters and asked for directions.

They were advised to keep the area closed and were told other units were on their way. "Don't disturb anything. In fact, stay inside your cars until you see other police cars arriving unless you see a personal car pulling in. In that case, get out and make them leave after getting their identification," they were told by Detective Andrews who had taken their call.

The two patrolmen sat in their car until they heard the sirens of other units turning off the state road into the park.

The county coroner and other state police crime scene units pulled up into a grouping that reminded one of the older cops of when the wagon trains formed a circle at night to fight off the Indians.

The two young recruits led the men to where they could just see the body snagged on a limb. It appeared from the bank to be in a bad stage of decomposition.

"Don't disturb this scene. You two young recruits, yes you, both of you, walk around here and collect anything that could possibly be evidence and put each piece into a separate clear plastic evidence bag and label it. Watch your step. Don't step on anything that might be useful." Detective Andrews advised the younger guys.

"What about this cigarette butt?" one questioned Andrews.

"I said bag everything. That includes a cigarette butt," Detective Andrews told them.

The new recruits did as they were told. There was not a lot of evidence other than natural disturbances caused by flooding to collect.

They did find where a small fire had been built and had the presence of mind to stir through the charred ashes.

Inside those ashes they found one tiny scrap of pink material and another tiny piece of some kind of white material, so that too was bagged and labeled. The scrap of cloth might have been overlooked since it did not seem possible a homosexual male would be wearing pink. They had no idea what the white material was but bagged it too. But the recruits were diligent and saved the scraps.

By this time a couple of state conservation officers had arrived on the scene with one's flat bottom boat on top of their car to assist in the recovery.

They were given assistance in getting the boat into the water and then the boat was tied off to a tree with a long rope.

The CO's paddled the small boat out to where they could get a better look at what was hung up on the half-submerged tree limb. It was for sure a body and appeared to be that of a very small person, perhaps that of a child.

The tissues had been under water so long that a lot of the flesh was missing, probably falling prey to catfish, turtles, carp or other wild game or simply natural decomposition.

The COs gently removed the body and laid the remains inside the bottom of the boat on a sheet they had brought for that purpose and secured it with ropes. They then paddled back to the side of the bank where they stepped out and helped the others drag the boat and its grisly cargo up the side of the muddy bank.

At that point, the county coroner stepped forward to take charge of the scene.

After gently turning the remains over and looking at all angles of it, he determined it was most likely a female body, and said it appeared to be a girl about nine or ten years old.

This fact nearly stopped Detective Andrews' heart. The only missing child he knew of was Sally Quinn. Could this be that little girl, he mused.

The crime scene technicians scoured the scene a second time for clues but found nothing overlooked by the two young recruits. After taking numerous photographs of the body and the surrounding scene they gently wrapped the remains in a white sheet and inserted their grisly package into a zippered body bag in preparation for taking it to the local university hospital for an autopsy.

Detective Andrews said, "Let's get her to the ME and find out who she is and what killed her. Maybe we can get a better clue once we know how she died."

One of the conservation officers decided he would like to use the restroom before he left the area. He had a key to unlock the doors which had been under lock and key to try to deter the park's usage.

Inserting his key in one of the doors he stumbled backward and yelled for assistance.

"There is something dead in here," he yelled. "Phew, what a stink."

Other officers came behind the CO and covering their lower faces with their handkerchiefs, entered the bathroom.

At first, they could see nothing out of place but all of them knew this is where a dead animal or body was located.

They checked both stalls and then saw the trash can in the corner.

Lifting the lid gingerly, the officer jumped backwards and said, "There, I told you there was something dead inside here."

Crammed down inside the trash can was the body of a child, or at least most of the skeleton of one.

They exited the building and called their superiors on the telephone asking the coroner and the crime scene people to return to the site because they had found a second body.

The coroner's wagon proceeded on to the hospital with its burden, but all the others turned around and returned to the scene. The coroner would return after dropping off his burden at the hospital.

Placing a clean sheet on the floor and placing gloves on their hands, they removed the small body by turning the can gingerly on its side and sliding the remains out onto a sheet. Not much was left of it. Heat and time had done its damage, but there was enough skin on the chest of the victim to tell a sad tale. The officers saw what they believed was a burn on the left side of the chest.

Remembering that the child's body they had just pulled from the water only a short time before, they recalled that it too had a burn mark on the left side of its chest.

"The same perp did both of these little kids," Officer Darren Andrews said.

After exhaustive examination of the body and bagging up every cigarette butt or any other material located inside the restroom, this second body was also removed to the morgue for autopsy and the locks were put back into place on the outer side of the restroom doors.

CHAPTER SEVEN

The medical examiner talked with Detective Andrews as she made the long Y cut to the girl's body that would open it up for her inspection.

Detective Andrews always stood by when one of his cases was being autopsied. He wanted to be there and know everything he could about every victim he brought to the ME's office.

"I can tell you right now what killed this little girl, and yes, it is a girl," the ME said.

Prior to making the big "Y" incision on the body she had looked at it for over half an hour through a magnifying lens. What that inspection told her surprised even her because she originally thought the cause of death might be hard to spot on a body that was in this state of decomposition.

"This child was manually strangled," she told Detective Andrews and she pointed to the spot in the child's throat that still contained massive bruising. "Someone with very strong hands choked the life out of her."

The remainder of the examination would take up much of the rest of her day and when the forensic sample results were returned to her in a few days or weeks, she was sure it could contain some surprising information also.

The first thing the ME pointed out to Detective Andrews was the burned area around the left breast of the young girl.

"That looks to me like a cigarette burn," she told him. "That bastard put his cigarette out on her little breast!"

When she had exposed the inner throat lining of the child and had taken a swab and placed the material on a slide, she was sure what she had gotten was a semen sample. The same was true for the vagina and rectal area. This little girl had been raped many times. Her stomach is full of semen. Now if they could just get the DNA of any suspects, they might be able to identify her killer and cinch the case.

The ME was also going to send the cigarette butts recovered at the scene to the FBI for DNA analysis. She was pretty sure she had recovered some DNA from the cigarette butt.

"Do you have a suspect now?" the ME asked Detective Andrews. "If you do have one, may I be the first to put my hands around his own throat," she fumed.

'Yes, we do. We have one man in jail. If I can get a court order for a DNA swab inside his mouth, would that be sufficient to help you," he asked her.

"Yes, it definitely would. I am also going to send the cigarette butts to the lab and this tiny scrap of pink material and the tiny bit of white paper-like material.

"I think the scrap of white paper might be the remains of a coffee filter, but we will have to wait for the results to come back. This indicates to me something to do with making drugs. Does that fit with your analysis of the case so far," the ME asked?

"Do you know what the girl was wearing when she disappeared?"

"Yes, I do, she was wearing blue jean shorts and a white blouse with pink flowers on it."

"When do you plan to do the autopsy of the other body," Detective Andrews asked the ME.

"I was going to wait until tomorrow to do that one, the ME said, "but after seeing that burn mark on the little girl's chest I think I will do the other one now."

The little girl's body was placed back in the refrigerated cooler and the second little body was placed on the now sterile table for review.

"Look, there is another burn area on this one's chest also. If the body had been inside that waste container much longer we probably would not have been able to see that," the ME said. "But a burn leaves a hard piece of flesh, much like a scar underneath the skin so this part was preserved a bit longer."

"The same person killed both of these children. There is just no doubt," the ME stated.

Detective Andrews went before Judge Rosenbaum and was given permission to have the ME take a swab sample from the inside of the prisoner's cheek.

This was done that afternoon and all the slides and body tissues needed for samples were hand carried by Detective Andrews to the police lab.

By pushing for speed, only two weeks later he was notified of an amazing coincidence.

The DNA on the cigarette stubs and the DNA found inside each of the children's body orifices matched perfectly proving what the ME had said during the autopsy, but there was no match to the sample taken from his prisoner.

Rapidly reaching a conclusion he could no longer deny, Detective Andrews rushed into the cell where his prime suspect had been residing for some time at the county's expense and demanded to know why he had confessed to the crime of abducting and killing that little girl.

"Do you realize that by confessing you have delayed the hunt for the perpetrator all this time?" he ranted.

The suspect finally admitted that he had lied. "I just wanted everyone to know my name."

Disgustedly Detective Andrews yelled for the jailer to come and release the man from his cell.

Wanting very badly to use his fists on the man, he strove to contain his temper.

"We are not through with you yet," Detective Andrews told him as he shook his finger at the man who was no longer a suspect.

"I am going before the prosecutor right now and I am going to file as many charges as I can think up against you. There is the charge of false informing, obstruction of justice and several others I can think of. I hope when you come before Judge Rosenbaum that he throws the book at you," he snarled to the man as he walked away.

Now the chase to find the killer had to start from scratch once again.

But the identity of the one victim had been confirmed. The child found in the water was young Sally's and the body was released to the family for burial. They still did not yet know the identity of the second body.

Trained counselors were brought in to Sally's school to aid the students who had known the young girl and/or the young boy who was not yet identified.

People from all over the country began sending money to the family to use as it saw fit as soon as the story made the national news about the suspect who was no longer a suspect.

Soon there was almost $100,000 in donations in the local bank to help the family of this child.

After the girl's funeral expenses were paid there were tens of thousands of dollars left in the kitty.

The newspaper editor, Sallianne Carmichael, suggested that a memorial be erected in the town to honor the elementary school youngsters.

The editor had written some scathing editorials about the case against the man accused of killing her, but had not done so, who had stood in the way to the police finding the real killer.

"I believe they should bring back hanging, and let him dangle from a tree limb on the town's courthouse square," was the way she had concluded one of her editorials.

Friends of the little girl and other townspeople suggested that a skate park and playground be built on the school's grounds in her name with the remaining donated money.

The town's only design architect submitted drawings of his proposed playground and skate park with a castle theme play area which were presented to the town council for approval.

With the help of hundreds of volunteers over the following few weeks, a beautiful playground addition emerged to honor this child. Now every time another child goes out to play in the school's grounds they are reminded of the young girl, Sally—who would never grow up—but had also taught them all a bitter lesson.

"Never trust, talk to or ride with a stranger," was the theme of what these other children had learned the hard way.

Perhaps in dying Sally had saved the lives of some of her many young friends.

But the push was on now to identify the second body they had found.

All they knew at this point was that the second body was that of a very young boy, perhaps six or seven years old but no children had been reported missing since Sally's disappearance.

But it was a sure thing that the same person had killed both children. DNA results had proven that, now all the police needed to do was find the killer.

That would not be an easy job and would take up every minute of Detective Darren Andrew's future time until both cases were solved.

CHAPTER EIGHT

"Someone has to know who this little boy is," Detective Andrews fumed to the men and women who had been assigned to work with him in solving the cases. "He has to have had a parent somewhere, but who was he?"

None of those who were helping him do the footwork could answer Detective Andrews.

"How can we have a little boy killed, stuffed into a waste basket like a piece of trash in a public restroom for several weeks and no one report a child missing," he mused." This whole case just does not make sense."

"We knew from the start that the little girl was most likely Sally because she was reported missing by her mother, but no one has stepped forward and reported this child missing. What kind of people do we have in this town anyway?"

"Maybe the boy didn't live around here. Maybe he was from another area and was just dropped off here," one of the female officers proposed.

"No, I do not think that is so, but you could go through all the missing children files that we have and see if one this age and size has been reported missing anywhere else. But I am betting, since the same person is responsible for both deaths, that that person is local and known by many others," Detective Andrews said. "It would be a wild and unbelievable coincidence to make this two different people killing kids in exactly the same way. No, it is just one person involved."

"Jerry," Detective Andrews said to the young officer who had recently been assigned to assist him, "Go through all our files again. There has to be a clue that we are overlooking."

Jerry rose from his chair and went out the door and down to the missing person's desk to sort through the small file one more time.

While knowing in his heart ahead of time he would not find a missing person report that fit this kid, he began looking at the profiles of all the other missing persons.

For some reason he could not explain, Jerry kept coming back to the file that the director of Children of Eden Ranch had filed for the little boy who had been at their camp but had been reclaimed by his mother.

"I wonder where that woman went," he thought to himself. "Did she just run away and take her little boy with her?"

"Or, could this young boy be the one that the COE director had said he left for a visit with his mother?"

Something about that whole case just had never made sense to anyone within the department. Maybe it was time to take a closer look inside that file.

He closed the file and took it back with him to Detective Andrew's office and plopped it on his superior's desk, saying, "I'll bet you my next paycheck that this little boy is the one we found. I have no way of knowing that, but I have learned to trust my gut instincts."

"We don't know where his mother is either. We have only the word of the COE director that he left the little boy at his mother's house while he visited the various churches that day. He has never claimed to have seen the boy's mother, just someone on the house's porch. Maybe we need to do some interviews with those church people again. Maybe they can put us onto the right track."

According to the director's report, he dropped the little boy off at his mother's house about 9 a.m. Someone on the porch hugged the little boy, swung him around, kissed him and told him how much he had been missed. But when the director arrived back that evening to pick up the boy, not a soul could be found inside that house.

"I remember when we went out there to check the place out, after this report was filed, that it looked like no one had been in that house in a long time," Detective Andrews said. "Did that preacher man lie to us?"

"Let's go out there and take one more look around. Maybe we missed something before that will make more sense to us now."

So saying, both officers grabbed their hats and headed out to the outskirts of town to the little yellow house where Billy and his mother had lived and from where both of them had disappeared.

But on the way to that house the men were dispatched to another small house in a town about ten miles distant where another child's body had just been found.

Slapping the Kojak light onto the top of their cruiser the investigators lost no time in arriving at their new destination.

An officer from the small town's tiny police department was

waiting for Detective Andrews on the front porch of that house and led them inside when they mounted the steps being careful to avoid stepping on some bloodstains.

"What do we have here?" Detective Andrews asked the young pimply-faced recruit.

"A woman called our station house about a half hour ago to say she had arrived home from work and had found her eight-year-old daughter dead in her bedroom, and the babysitter out cold on the floor inside the house with a severe head injury. The ambulance has already transported that young girl to the emergency room for treatment.

"I have put the mother in my patrol car and I have not walked into the room where the little girl is lying. She is in that second bedroom on the left. As far as I know, only the mother has been inside that room."

"Good, you did exactly as you should have done. Now go outside and string up some Crime Scene tape and keep everyone away from here except for those that have to be here to investigate this crime," Detective Andrews told the young man who immediately left to do as he was told.

The two remaining officers stepped carefully into the room where they could see the naked body of the young girl. They were careful not to touch anything nor to step on any evidence but they needed to touch her throat to make sure she was dead.

As they touched her neck they could feel that she was dead and they noticed also, the burn on her left breast.

"That madman has struck again and left his trademark burn," Detective Andrews cried.

The officers left the room and radioed in for assistance and confirmed to the dispatcher that a body had been found and identified by the mother.

"Go outside there and talk to her mother," Detective Andrews advised Officer Jerry Marlow. "Find out her name, age, the last time the mother saw her alive. Get as much information as you can so we can move quickly on this one."

Detective Andrews knew exactly what he would find when the child's naked body was turned onto its back, but that could wait until the coroner arrived and the crime scene photographer. He did not want to be accused later of damaging or contaminating the evidence.

Officer Marlow returned inside to speak with his boss. "I learned some interesting things about this young girl from her mother," he said.

"She is a violin virtuoso and at only seven years old, has already stunned a wide range of audiences around the world with her musical ability.

"That violin lying busted in the corner is a specially made violin, made just for her by one of the finest violin makers in the world.

"No one knows why he made the violin for her and gave it to her for free unless he was so stunned by her performance that he knew only she could do justice to his own handiwork.

"The world lost a great violinist today when this child was killed. At this young age she had already played for the US president and kings and queens around the world. She was an amazing young girl to say the very least."

Already heavy in heart, Detective Andrews could only shake his head.

The fine violin was now a piece of broken wood that had been kicked across the room and lay in tatters held together only by its strings.

Did you find out anything about the other little girl who was supposed to be babysitting this one?

"Yes, I did.

"She is 14 years old and was hired to come here after school and tend the younger child. She has worked here for over a year now and the two were great friends, the child's mother told me.

"Most of the time she arrived within minutes of this one getting off the school bus. They would have a sandwich and a glass of milk together, then the violinist would begin practicing.

"It was an enjoyable friendship for both the girls. While the virtuoso practiced for an hour or so, the older girl would do her own homework, so it worked out well for both of them. She would stay until the girl's mother arrived home from work and then walk the short distance back to her own home."

"This child's name is Abigail Swanson and she is seven years old and in the second grade at the local elementary school unless she is on a concert tour and during that time she has a tutor."

While the officers reviewed the scene and waited for the crime scene wagon to arrive the crowd outside the home continued to grow, with about 75 persons now standing around in the yard outside and kept there by the crime scene ribbons.

The officers made sure that the steps and front porch area was protected from footprints since there were smears of blood in those areas.

It was also obvious that something had been dragged across the yard because the grass was slightly higher than usual and had been flattened by whatever had been dragged.

Curiosity seekers talked among themselves wondering especially about what had happened inside the modest dwelling.

It would have been interesting to know if the officers realized that the killer was also among that group of onlookers. Like many types of criminals, he had returned to the scene of his crime and watched the police officers do their job.

He had parked his old white pickup back behind some trees on an old logging road that ran not far from the house that he had been casing each afternoon looking to find this child alone for some time now.

Each afternoon he made sure to be in the bushes when the little girl got off her school bus.   The older girl was not to his liking and he was anxious to try out the young child.   He liked them very young and vulnerable and believed the older girls could possibly overtake or hurt HIM.

He had waited there for several days waiting for an opportunity to abduct this particular girl if only one girl got off the school bus—he decided to take advantage of this opportunity.

He had often heard her playing her "fiddle" as he thought snidely of her musical instrument, but he was not impressed by her ability. Instead, he was impressed by her age and her looks. It had not been difficult to sneak into her house once he saw that her babysitter had not arrived with her or just after her.

But as he began crossing the yard to the home, the young babysitter showed up but did not see him. Instead, she was intent on looking at a flower bed that was in full bloom. She could hear her charge inside the house already practicing and knew by that that she was OK.

As she stood looking down intently into a fully opened hibiscus flower, he had sneaked up behind her and hit her over the head with a fairly large piece of wood he had picked up off a wood pile by the side of the house.

As she had fallen to the ground, the scumbag had kicked her in the ribs and about her head several times with his steel-toed boots, then had dragged her behind the flowering bush to conceal her from passers-by on the road.

He had run up the steps of the house on his tiptoes and slipped inside the unlocked screen door. He knew the beautiful young girl had not heard him because her music never stopped.

Slipping up to the door of the bedroom that she used for practicing, he peeked around the corner and could hardly believe his luck. She stood there in the center of the room with her eyes closed and with her back to him.

 It had been a simple matter to take a giant step inside the room and place a hand over her mouth to keep her from screaming.

As she became aware there was someone inside the room with her, Abigail Swanson had dropped her precious instrument. Fearing that it was damaged, she attempted to free herself so she could pick it up, but that just infuriated her attacker more.

At that point, he had stomped his big foot down on the instrument, crushing it, then had kicked it into a corner to lie there as he ravished the young girl's body, over and over again.

Once he had completed his dirty work and had peeked outside to make sure no one knew he was there, he had lighted his ritual cigarette. After smoking it down almost to the filter's end, he placed the still burning ember onto the girl's left breast to extinguish it then dropped it onto the floor.

Replacing his clothing and making sure he had not left any clues behind he slipped from the house, crossed the yard and returned to his vehicle parked on the logging road.

It had been a simple matter to move his pickup to where everyone else's were parked, then mingle with the other onlookers to determine just how everyone was feeling about the killing.

You could plainly see where the other girl had dragged herself across the yard, up the steps on her belly and across the porch floor.

It had been difficult for her to open the door and enter the house on her belly because she was afraid she would be attacked again, but she knew she must see if her little friend Abigail was all right.

She was the first to see the carnage inside the bedroom and her friend lying on the floor. As she dragged herself back across the floor to reach the telephone, it started ringing.

On the other end of the line was the child's mother checking with her to make sure all was well. It had been that mother who had called the police and ambulance and headed home to find her talented daughter dead and the babysitter nearly so.

Mrs. Swanson had arrived home only minutes after the state police arrived and would have rushed into her home to check on her daughter except that Detective Andrews prevented her from entering the house.

"No, Mrs. Swanson, "I'm sorry but you cannot come inside right now. I will make sure that your daughter's death is handled with dignity.

"Please go back over there and sit in your car. As soon as it is possible to let you inside your home, I will personally come outside and get you," he promised her.

Weeping softly, she obeyed the officer, knowing that for now her daughter belonged to him. She also realized that she must do everything possible to assist in solving her daughter's murder and if that meant she could not see her little girl immediately, she knew she would eventually be able to do so. She believed the officer, whom she didn't know, had told her truthfully that he would get her when she could see her daughter's face again.

Heartsick, she returned to her vehicle and took a seat, only then noticing that hundreds of her fellow townspeople were gathered in her yard to lend support and find out the details.

It seemed only minutes before she saw that some young persons were quietly coming forth and placing floral bouquets in a pile near her flower bed that the babysitter had been admiring when she was struck down. I wonder how they found out so fast? she pondered.

Among the mementos were tiny violins tied with ribbons attached to the long stems of flowers; there were also teddy bears and Raggedy Anne dolls that so many of her fellow townspeople knew the little girl loved.

The young girl may have already been famous and had traveled the world, but she was still "theirs" and they wished to honor her.

Only a few hours later, news vans from every news station in the country would be on this street with big white dishes mounted on their trucks broadcasting the news of this particular child's death to the world.

Hordes of newscasters were battling for position to do their updates with the view of the small house of tragedy and the triumph of this small child behind them.

Telegrams began arriving almost before Abby's body had been removed from the house.

The president of the United States was one of the first to send his condolences. He and his wife had asked the little girl to play her violin at a state dinner he had recently held for several heads of state.

Queen Elizabeth of England had been so entranced with Abby that the girl and the queen had formed an instant bond of friendship.

The child had no living grandmothers, all of them having died long before her own birth, so as she had looked at the Queen she imagined how her grandmothers might have looked.

After playing the violin until the queen was crying with joy, the tiny little girl cozied up to her and asked her not to cry. "I love you and I did not mean to make you cry," the child had told the queen.

Flustered because she was not generally so openly affectionate with her own grandchildren, the queen had been so overcome with joy in the little girl that she had drawn her little body close to her own and hugged her.

"I'm not crying because I'm sad," the queen told Abby. "I'm crying because you make me so happy. That is what moms, grandmoms and other women do when they are happy. They cry."

The telegram extending her condolences almost got to Abby's mom before the president's had done.

All over the world, leaders would bow their heads in prayer for the loss of this one tiny girl from an even tinier town somewhere in the Midwestern part of the United States.

Abby was not only a national treasure, her talent was a world treasure and the whole world would mourn her passing, especially in such a gruesome way.

Detective Andrews wanted to be present at the autopsy of this child.

He stood across the table from the medical examiner who had to fight back tears as she made the initial Y incision to see what depravities this child had endured.

After spending long hours meticulously examining every part of her little body, the ME slammed down her scalpel and removed her gloves and threw everything on the exam table.

"I hate this job. I hate to see the vicious ways in which people can be killed, especially a small child," she exclaimed.

"This child is the victim of the same rapist/killer that has been killing the other children," she told Detective Andrews.

'She has been raped in every manner possible, beaten and then killed. This just makes no sense at all.

"It is impossible to think about someone killing this little girl who had so much to offer this mixed up world.

"Prodigy's like her are only born about every 200 years. Why would someone kill her?" the ME sobbed.

Detective Darren Andrews had tears in his own eyes as he commiserated with the ME.

"I don't understand the futility of someone killing her either, but I swear before God that I will catch the bastard and put him away for the rest of his life.

"The death penalty would be too easy for him. I want him to be put in a prison with some tough guys who will very quickly show him what they can do to a child rapist/killer."

As soon as Detective Andrews returned to his office, he called in all those who had been assisting him in trying to find the killer of the children who had each died a horrible death after an even worse torture at the hands of this devil.

He wished he could call back in the man who had admitted to the torture killing but he knew this was not an option. That man had lied and caused a serious delay in apprehending the real criminal.

This happens more often than those outside the police ranks could imagine. What excitement they get out of doing this happens regularly in police work and Detective Andrews believed they should be punished severely by the court systems.

After all those involved in the murders were assembled in his office, he turned to them and spoke rapidly.

"This case is not closed. It never will be as long as I am alive, I swear I will get this person if it is the last thing I ever do," he said.

"I want to talk to you about another angle we have just been learning about. This new term you will be hearing regularly is "face recognition."

We will need some of you to be proficient in using the computer to its utmost. Some of us never use one so we cannot be of much help to you.

What we are going to do is check every business near these abductions to see if they had a camera mounted outside their locations that might have captured the onlookers who may be seen from more than one angle.

"I really believe that this person we seek may be just the type of person who might return to the scene of his crime and watch the police comb the premises around the murder for clues to what happened."

'He is probably thinking he got away with murder, but I'm here to tell you that he is not going to get away with it," Detective Andrews said.

"There are several computer programs available and several information technology experts who can help us try to identify this person if he appears in more than one scene."

"I have asked these IT people to come here, install the systems, explain to you what we may be able to obtain from the computer systems. The first IT person will be here bright and early Monday morning, so get some rest this weekend and be ready to learn and shine on Monday.

"I would also like to include news reporter Sallianne Carmichael in this group. She has been very helpful to us in the past because of her own ethics in printing news stories about crime scenes. You all know her, I believe"

Some of those people who would be doing most of the grunt work on the computer got together and thought about what they might be actually looking for when they studied these tapes.

"Wouldn't it be great if we saw the same man in more than one group of onlookers, one young female said. I would love to be the one to locate him."

As this smaller group departed Detective Andrews's office they became very excited about perhaps being the one to recognize this perp.

Bright and early Monday morning, Detective Andrews was in the office by 5 A.M. trying to assimilate all that he wanted to transmit to his group of younger officers.

"We cannot depend on being the one to recognize this man," Detective Andrews explained to his troops when they began to arrive. We could be wrong. Our eyes may fail us. We need it on tape on the computer.

"That would demand that each of us be perfect in our facial recognition. But if the computer system is as good as the person told me it was, the computer will peer closely at every person standing around the crime scene.

"It will record that man's face and move on to the people in the next tape, one after another, until it has seen and recorded every person in each scene shown on those tapes the businesses will loan to us.

"As it looks at scene one, the computer will eyeball every person in the second tape and those at the next crime scene, etc. etc." he explained to his young troops.

"When it gives us a flag on any person on both tapes at both crime scenes, then we may be able to identify that person and make an arrest. We must get him off the streets of our town to keep our children safe," Detective Andrews explained.

"Wouldn't it be great if the computer can come up with a facial match right away?"

"And it would also be a miracle," one of the young officers replied.

"OK, let's go. There is an IT specialist to sit with each one of you. This IT specialist will step in whenever you think you have something for us to go on."

Separating quickly, these young experts were anxious to get started and maybe be the one who could solve these crimes.

But several days would go by before any miracle was announced by Detective Andrews.

"Well, troops, we have struck it rich here. We now have a prime suspect who appeared in two tapes at two crime scenes. Now all we have to do is identify this man, bring him in for questioning, and throw him in jail."

The gang that had been working so hard wanted to know which group had found the same man in two tapes at two crime scenes. What he looked like and if anyone could put a name to him was the next big test of this new computer system.

One of the members of this young group thought he might recognize the man or at least be able to give his superior officer a clue.

"I think I saw that guy in a big truck, pulling a wagon load of baled hay at the violinist's crime scene.

"I was one of the officers at the scene up at the park where the little girl was found dead in the little creek. I and a friend picked up all the evidence we could find at the scene and bagged it, but I did not see this guy on the tapes at that scene. But he could be the one.

"At the scene where the violinist was murdered, he walked up to the crowd and asked what was going on and he looked right straight at the unseen camera as he said it. I think the camera got a really good look at him. He could have parked his truck and hay (if he was hauling hay that day) and walked up to the crowd. Just might be a shot in the dark or it might be a real clue," he concluded.

"That's wonderful information that we did not have at either of the times in question. Perhaps you are the winner of this particular contest," Detective Andrews said.

The image of the man they were talking about was blown up and put on a large screen at the front of the hall for everyone to view to see if they could recognize him.

"I don't really have a name for him, but he often buys hay from the farmers around here," one woman said.

"I have heard from these farmers that the man in question works at the Children of Eden Ranch in the next county up from ours."

'Detective Andrews said, "Let's go people. Let's get this man off the street. We will start with this children's ranch and go from there."

The officers piled into each of their cruisers and set off to go the 25 miles or so to this ranch. Each held in their hand a copy of the computer image of this man.

Arriving at the ranch, they asked to see the director and he was called from his office to meet with the police.

"Do you recognize this man?" Detective Andrews asked the director.

"Yes, I do," the man responded warmly. "Why do you want him?" "What has he done?"

Officer Andrews explained that the police in Johnson County were looking for the person who had killed several children in their area, after torturing them, abusing them, then killing them.

"Oh, you must be mistaken, this man has worked for me for several months on a volunteer basis, and he has never been in trouble before."

"I assure you we are not mistaken. He was seen at the scene of two of the crimes and was identified by computer experts and our own officers," Detective Andrews advised Daddy Tom.

"Bring him in here. Go with this man and bring him in," Detective Andrews told two of his men, and don't take your eyes off the man."

The suspect was brought in from the barn where he had been feeding the horses the children were allowed to ride in their "happy time".

Happy time was when they were not in a classroom, or the gardens and orchards, and were not needed anywhere else on the campus of the Children of Eden Ranch.

"Please state your name and age and give us a synopsis of what type of work you have done in the past. Have you ever been arrested? If so, what were your charges? There is no need to lie to us because we can track you down within ten minutes or so. Start speaking."

The suspect gave his name as Johnathan Coats, age 45, and said he had always worked in a factory and had owned several homes at one time. He said he had given a home to each of his half-dozen ex-wives so they would not have to make house payments after he divorced them or they divorced him, since each of the homes were free and clear of a mortgage.

"Were you ever arrested for anything?" Detective Andrews asked him.

"No sir, I have never even had a speeding ticket," he responded.

"Have you ever worked in places where children were housed?"

"Only here at the ranch," the suspect said.

"Do you work closely with these children? Do you like children?"

"Yes, I work closely with these children. I have to supervise when they are riding the horses. I also have to saddle them up for the kids. I allow them to help me feed and water those horses they have grown to love."

"Why are you asking me all these questions?" the perp asked.

"We are asking because we have you on tape at two of the children's torture/murders," Andrews explained.

"No, way. I haven't been near any of those crime scenes. Someone is lying about me."

"Nope, we have you on two tapes at different crime scenes and one person who was also there fingered you as a possible suspect. The computer experts also compared your facial expressions at each of the scenes. Your ass is fried," Detective Andrews told Mr. Coats. "Let's go, put your hands behind your back. Cuff him young man, and put the chain around his waist", Detective Andrews told the man who had made the facial recognition.

"We have our man." Andrews stated.

On the way to the jail for further interrogation, Detective Andrews phoned the young reporter, Sallianne, and told her what was going down.

She assured him she would be at the jail before he got there, and she was.

Sallianne immediately shot a picture of the perp on her camera/phone for use in her stories about this case.

She was relieved that this man who had tortured and murdered these young people was finally in custody She secretly hoped he would get the chair. Anything less would not be a harsh enough penalty for this man. He deserved to die if anyone ever had deserved it.

Sallianne would follow this case closely and report on it fairly, giving great praise to Detective Andrews for his good work and for the work of his new "IT" personnel.

CHAPTER NINE

Arriving at the jail, the perp was shoved into a chair inside an interrogation room.

There were three officers inside the room also and several more were in an adjacent room watching events through a one-way mirror on the wall. The handcuffs were still in place on his wrists attached to a chain around his waist just in case he tried to cause trouble.

A tape recorder was placed on the table before the perp so every word he uttered could be heard on that tape when he went to trial and there was no doubt he would go on trial if inmates did not kill him prior to his trial on the abduction, torture and murder charges which he now faced.

My name is Johnathan Coats; my age is 45, and I have no address because I have been living at the Children of Eden Ranch since it opened. I believe you have their address already. Since I never receive mail, I can't recall their exact address.

Detective Andrews opened the interrogation by asking Mr. Coats what he was doing in Stoneville on July 13, 2015 when young Sally had disappeared and had not been found until weeks later because the one man they thought had committed the murder did not kill anybody.

He merely slowed down the investigation by saying he had committed the crime. She was found several weeks afterwards, having been partially eaten by animals and fish in a small stream feeding into a river located north of where she had lived her entire life.

Mr. Coats denied he was at the scene of her abduction in July.

"Now, Mr. Coats, we know you were at the scene because we have taped proof that you were there," Detective Andrews told him.

After several hours of talking with the officers, Mr. Coats finally admitted he had stopped in that little town that day to ask the crowd what was going on.

He had shuddered when someone in the crowd told him about the abduction and killing of the virtuoso violinist.

He would never admit that day or on any day after that that he had any other motive for stopping at the scene of her abduction.

Detective Andrews moved on with his questioning.

Mr. Coats, can you tell us what you were doing on September 15, 2015, when you told someone in a crowd of people that you were hauling hay for your horses?

"I was hauling hay back to the COE Ranch," he replied.

Where was your truck when you appeared at the scene of this crime, he was asked.

"There was such a lot of people standing around that I had to leave my truck and trailer load of hay back a few paces because there was no room nearby to park and I might have hit someone there were so many standing around.

I never did find what was going on that day, so I went on back to the COE Ranch with my hay.

'Do you mean to tell us that you never heard about the young violin virtuoso who was murdered and her babysitter, nearly killed?

No, no one told me anything that day. That is why you have that picture of me on that tape.

'This little girl, who was so talented at so young an age was a personal friend of presidents and the Queen of England. Everyone wanted to see that she succeeded.

She was very young but she was one of the best-known talents that had emerged in perhaps 200 years. Only about once in a person's lifetime is there born a talent such as hers."

"Why did you kill her and why did you stomp on her expensive violin, which had been a gift to her from the Queen of England, after she was sent for and played that same violin for the Queen.

"And, another thing that same day, why did you attempt to kill the 14-year-old girl whom you struck over her head with a stick of wood?

"This child survived but had to spend weeks and weeks in the hospital and rehab unit to overcome the damage you did to her head.

"How did you get away from that scene without the tape showing you sneaking away," Detective Andrews asked.

"I didn't sneak away. I just walked out the back door, across the yard and back to my truck and returned to the COE Ranch," Mr. Coats replied.

"Mr. Coats, do you realize that you have just admitted you killed that young talented girl and nearly killed another one?"

"Yes, I realize that. I'm so sorry for those girls and the grief their families are going through.

"And, there is another one dead, a young boy, whom I also killed that I haven't told anyone about," Mr. Coats said.

"When did this one happen and who was this child, Mr. Coats? How and why did you kill this one."

"The third murder happened November 15, 2015. I found him alone in a home in this same little town. The mother was long gone and he was nearly starved, so I asked him to come with me.

"He came with me after I promised him I would feed him.

"I took him back up north where the first body was found. It was there that I raped him several times and then choked him to death. I left him in a trashcan inside the men's outside toilet."

Detective Andrews verified this man's story. and the body removed to the medical examiner's office for identification. There was very little of the boy's body left for the ME to examine since it had been a warm fall and he was inside the building out of the elements.

"Mr. Coats, can you tell us what you did with the body of the mother of this little boy?

"She has been missing just as long as the little boy was last seen and we have looked everywhere for her body."

"I guess I may as well tell you, I also killed her and dumped her body out in the swampy area west of that same town.

"I'm just glad you have got all of this out of my mind. I'm sorry for the deaths, but I just don't know what happens to me that makes me do these things," Mr. Coats replied.

"It is like something very evil, maybe a Devil lives inside my head and tells me to kill. It won't go away until I do. Please help me," he pleaded.

"I don't claim to have a halo over my head, I have some real problems," Mr. Coats said.

"Can you and will you, please show us where you dumped his mother's body. It would help her family to know she and her little boy are together again after all this time."

"Yes," was his only response.

"Take him away guys and put him in a squad car with handcuffs and chains on him. We do not want him to get away at this stage of the game," Detective Andrews said.

"Let's see if we can find the mother of this child and reunite them."

Several squad cars made the trip outside of town to the marshy area Mr. Coats had described.

It truly was marshy and most of the marsh had been searched looking for the little boy earlier in the year.

But Mr. Coats took them to the other, southern end, of the marsh and told them to stop.

"I think this is the place where I brought her. She was dead weight and I could not carry her very far, so I dragged her back a ways and left her back there.

"Follow me and I will show you," he told the police officers.

When they had walked several yards back into the swamp, which had narrow solid lanes criss-crossing the marshy areas Mr. Coats told them this was where he had left her body.

All the officers walked with each one having the back of another looking for a trace of the woman's body.

After much searching one of the officers told the others to stop. "I think I have found her remains," he said.

True enough, there was a pile of bones lying in plain sight on this narrow lane but little was left of it.

"Turtles, big ones I'll bet you," got to her first. Then once they were done chewing on her, probably coyotes or a pack of wild dogs finished her off. We are lucky there is anything left of her at all.

Detective Andrews radioed back to the station to get the coroner and the crime scene people out here and then gave the dispatcher precise coordinates where the corpse could be found.

Soon the swamp was a swarm with crime scene officers.

It would be hours later before the body was bagged, put on the gurney and taken to the MEs office located about 20 miles north.

An autopsy the day afterwards of the bones would validate everything Mr. Coats had admitted to and he was placed in a cell by himself for his own protection.

As in the prior procedures this ME did, she sent samples of several of the bones to a laboratory for final identification based on the DNA evidence.

It would be a couple of weeks later when the final identification of the bones which had been sent to the lab for DNA was returned.

The ME immediately called Detective Andrews to advise him that a really unusual thing had shown up on the DNA test.

"All these bones do not match," she advised him. "They show there were two different people in that pile of bones."

"Is he accused of murdering anyone else, or is someone else missing and not accounted for," she asked Detective Andrews.

"Yes, there is, there was another disappearance of young Billy's mother. She has never been located. How do we test her DNA," the detective asked the ME.

"If we had something from her home that might contain her DNA, perhaps that would work and you can solve all these cases, the ME advised him.

"If you can find her hairbrush or toothbrush, anything that might contain traces of DNA, those things would work.

'It also meant a return to the jail housing Mr. Coats, who at first refused to admit to killing Billy's mother, but finally he admitted to all.

Detective Andrews returned to the home of Billy and his mother and got lucky and found a hairbrush containing several hairs. No one else had lived in that house since Billy's mother disappeared so it was most likely the mother's brush.

DNA test on those hair samples confirmed the second pile of bones indeed belonged to Billy's mother. Now that crime was also solved.

"Mr. Coats now faced several charges of abduction, torture, murder, desecration of a corpse, rape and several other heinous crimes.

He would find himself in prison for a very long time and probably would be sentenced to death to boot.

The response to the news that the killer, kidnapper and other vile names had been arrested by Detective Darren Andrews and had admitted to performing these crimes caused the immediate inundation of cash to this small town. It amassed at such an amazing rate that a special account was opened at the local bank for safe-keeping.

Soon this account held more than a $100,000 and the question now was, "what do we do with all this money?"

Since two of the children were only 8-years-old and were in the same grade at the local elementary school, plans were made to take this money, which included a hefty check from the Queen of England, and build a really nice outdoor play area and skate park in remembrance of these children.

It took about a year from the time the plans were made until the play area and skate park were completed and today it remains a beautiful, functional focal point for the entire town.

And Mr. Coats remains in a lonely prison cell for his heinous crimes, locked away forever from the other inmates who have been known quite frequently to kill and badly maim child murderers.

Everyone involved with the cases cited here felt strongly that Mr. Coats should have received the death penalty. But most people involved in the case, felt he would suffer much, much more before he died, from the inmates if they could get to him.

The other inmates had nothing but time on their own hands. They could wait for an opportune time and let nature take its course with Mr. Coats.

Detective Andrews was promoted to police chief and Sallianne Carmichael won many awards for her treatment of these crimes in a sane and sensible manner.

Helen C. Ayers

ABOUT THE AUTHOR

For many years (20+) Mrs. Ayers was a police reporter, invited along with both the Indiana State Police investigators and the local Sheriff's Department as well as the Department of Drug Enforcement on their raids, to take pictures for both the officers and the newspaper she managed. She attended investigations on murders, arsons, drug raids and personal suicides, etc. to get first-hand information on which to write stories needed for the newspaper. It also provided her with many closely related ideas for actually writing books and providing her with data other writers may not have been exposed to when she expanded her writing to include murder mystery books. This book is one of two she has written.

During the Covid-19 pandemic during nearly all of 2020 she spent her time writing at the computer and completed this book; another book to read to children about Santa Claus and a dozen more books for children to be able to read themselves, each of which usually had a moral story about childhood safety at their center.

She was kept very busy during the pandemic not only with her writing, but caring for her husband as he was sent from cancer center, to hospitals, to nursing homes, undergoing several surgeries, etc. until he died on October 9, 2020. They had eloped when both were young and managed to successfully surf through 60+ years of marriage rearing two sons who are both ex-pats in Japan and Spain and the joy of grandparenthood with the addition of one of each, now both in their 30s.

Mrs. Ayers refused to have a picture of herself for this cover. She explained that her normally naturally curly hair had recently had the worst haircut of her entire life and did not want to advertise how awful it actually is. Maybe next time!